Royal Champions

By Catherine Hapka

Illustrated by the Disney Storybook Artists

New York

AN IMPRINT OF DISNEY BOOK GROUP

Printed in the United States of America

First Edition

1 3 5 7 9 10 8 6 4 2

Library of Congress Catalog Card Number: 2007909624
ISBN 978-1-4231-0928-0
For more Disney Press fun, visit www.disneybooks.com

Table of Contents

DISNEY'S THE LITTLE MERMAID

Ariel's Baby Beau

Ariel's new life on land was always full of surprises. One day, Eric told her he had something to show her, and he led her out to the stable.

"Surprise!" he exclaimed. Standing there was a cute little foal with long legs, big eyes, and the sweetest expression.

Ariel gasped. "It's a baby horse!" she cried. "Oh, he's adorable!"

"He's all yours," Eric said with a smile. "His name is Beau."

Ariel loved Beau right away. He loved her, too. She put a fancy
halter on him so she could lead him around everywhere.

She groomed him with his own jeweled brushes
until his coat gleamed.

She braided his short, soft mane.

"Doesn't he look beautiful?" Ariel asked Eric as Beau posed proudly.
"He certainly does!" Eric agreed.
Ariel's friend Scuttle the seagull was watching, too. "Fantabulicious!"
he declared.

Ariel played with her new little friend all day long. When night came, she couldn't bear to leave Beau alone in that big, cold stall.

"Maybe you'd better come inside for the night," she told him. "Just this once."

Grimsby and the other servants were quite surprised when Ariel led Beau into the castle. "Oh, dear," Grimsby said. "A horse in the house?"

"It's just for tonight," Ariel said with a smile. "Don't worry, he won't be any trouble at all."

She made Beau his own cozy bed near the fireplace. Soon he was all tucked in.

"Good night, little Beau." Ariel gave him a kiss on the nose. "Sleep tight!"

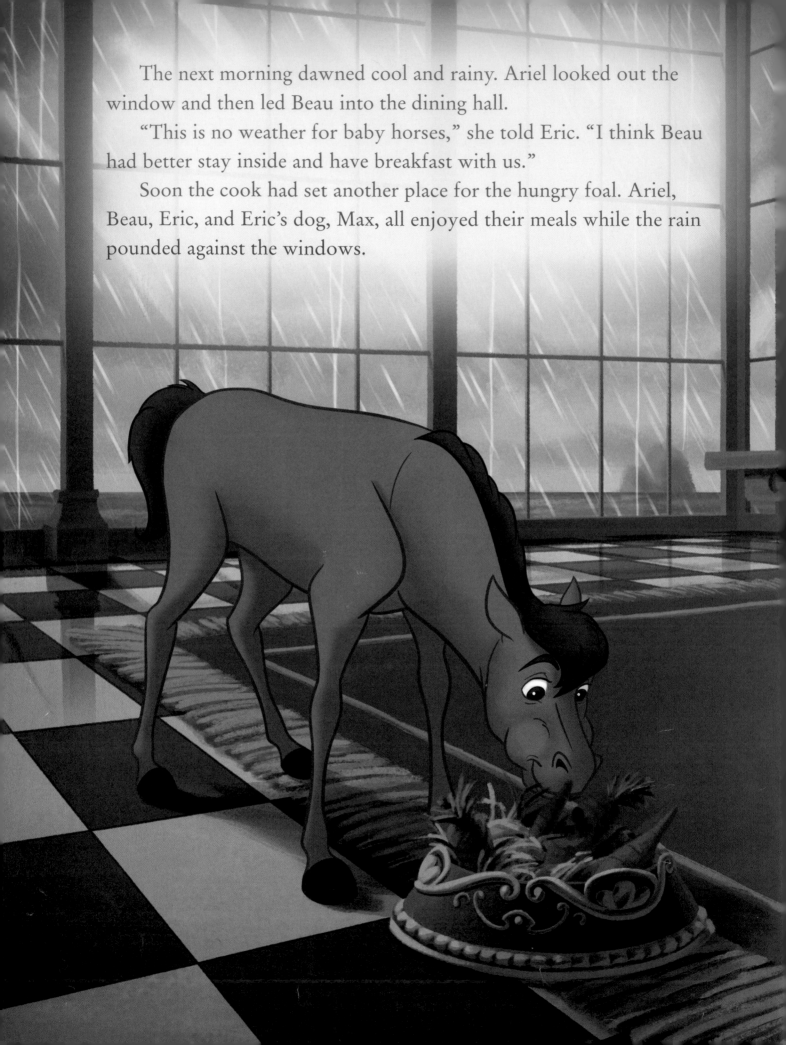

The next morning dawned cool and rainy. Ariel looked out the window and then led Beau into the dining hall.

"This is no weather for baby horses," she told Eric. "I think Beau had better stay inside and have breakfast with us."

Soon the cook had set another place for the hungry foal. Ariel, Beau, Eric, and Eric's dog, Max, all enjoyed their meals while the rain pounded against the windows.

When breakfast was over, it was still raining, so Ariel took Beau to play in the throne room. They both had lots of fun romping around together, and Beau was perfectly well behaved.

After all, he didn't
mean to break that vase . . .

Or leave hoofprints
all over the newly
washed floor . . .

Or eat the
houseplants. . . .

17

As the next few months passed, Ariel and Beau were hardly ever apart. Beau slept in the castle, ate in the dining room, and went everywhere with Ariel. Soon, all of the townspeople were used to seeing them together.

Ariel loved having Beau around. Not only was he cute—he was clever, too. She taught him to sit on his own special cushion in the throne room.

And before long, he could do more tricks than Max!

No matter what he was doing,
Beau would always come running
when Ariel called him.

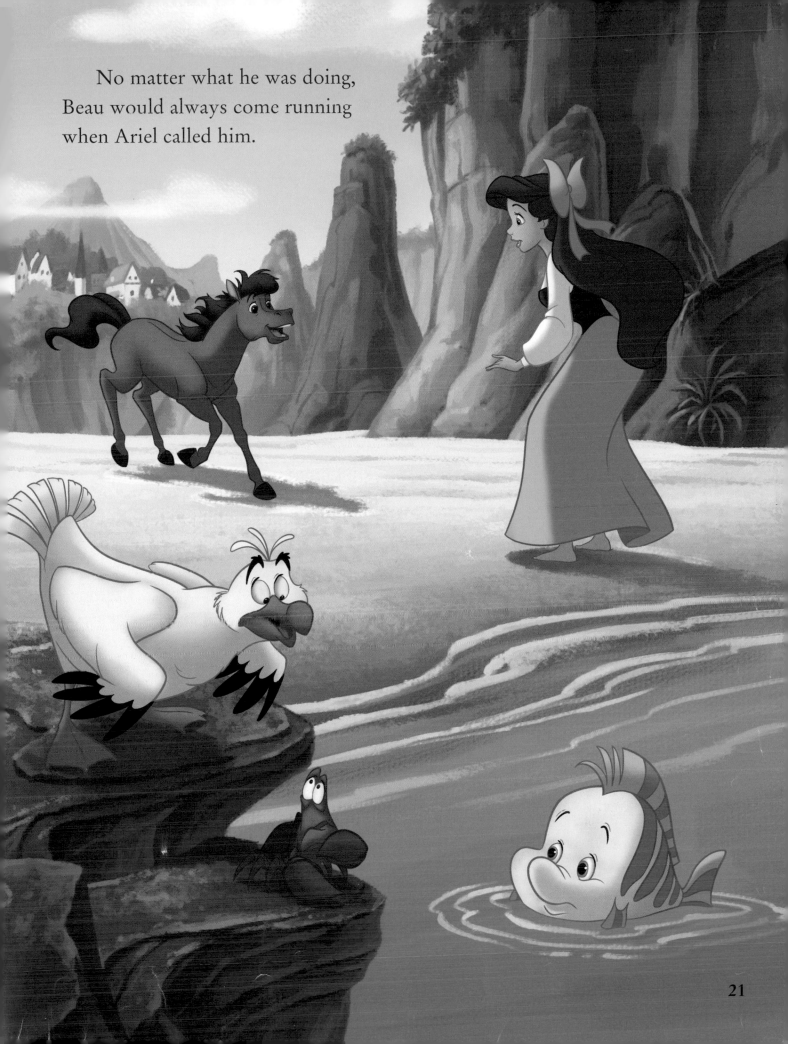

"You'd better be careful, Ariel," her friend Sebastian the crab warned one day. "Before long, that horse won't even know he's a horse anymore!"

Ariel laughed. "Don't be silly," she told Sebastian. "Besides, Beau's not a horse yet. He's just a baby!"

Beau *was* still young. But he was growing fast. It wasn't long before he started to have some trouble following Ariel around wherever she went.

Not long after that, the furniture started to collapse when Beau bumped into it.

Ariel wasn't too worried. She was happy just to spend her days with her sweet Beau.

The chef wasn't so pleased, though. He was running out of ideas for new recipes to serve the foal.

"For zis I went to zee school of cooking?" he grumbled as he served Beau yet another gourmet meal made out of grass, apples, and carrots.

One day, the entire castle was busy getting ready for a special occasion. The king and queen of a nearby kingdom were coming for a royal visit. Ariel and Eric wanted everything to be perfect.

At first, the visit *was* perfect. The king and queen were very nice when Ariel and Eric showed them around the palace.

"What a lovely castle," the queen said. "Such wonderful views!"

"Oh, yes," the king added. "And it's so peaceful and pleasant. Isn't it, dear?"

"Very peaceful," the queen agreed.

But the castle didn't stay peaceful for long. Suddenly, Beau burst in and galloped through the throne room—almost knocking over the guests!

"Oh, dear!" Ariel cried in alarm. "Beau, no!"

She could tell that Beau didn't mean any harm. But all at once, Ariel realized what it must look like to the guests. How many castles allowed a horse to play in their throne room? Beau was nearly grown up now. He was too big to stay inside.

"I'm so sorry, Your Majesties," Ariel told the visitors. "Beau doesn't know any better. This is all my fault."

But the king and queen didn't seem very upset. "It's quite all right, my dear," the queen said. "No harm done."

"Indeed," the king agreed. "We love horses. In fact, that reminds me—we brought you two a gift. Please come outside."

Ariel and Eric exchanged a glance. A gift? What could it be? They followed the visitors out of the castle. As usual, Beau tagged along.

"Surprise!" the queen exclaimed. "We hope you like her."

Ariel gasped. Standing in the courtyard was the prettiest little filly she'd ever seen.

Beau pranced forward to say hello. He and the filly made friends right away.

"She's beautiful," Eric said to the visitors. "Thank you—Ariel and I are honored by your generous gift."

Ariel smiled as she watched her horse get to know his new friend. "Yes, thank you very much. She's just perfect."

Soon the two young horses were happily grazing together in the pasture. And that night, instead of coming into the palace, Beau decided to stay outside.

"See?" Ariel told Eric with a smile. "I knew my Beau would realize he was a horse sooner or later!"

Sure enough, from that moment on, Beau *almost* always acted like a horse. Living in the castle with Ariel had been nice for a while, but he quickly learned that living the way other horses did was fun, too—especially when he got big enough to take Ariel for rides.

Ariel liked things better this way, as well. Beau had made a good house pet. But he made an absolutely wonderful horse!

Walt Disney's Sleeping Beauty

Buttercup the Brave

"Which horse would you like to ride today?" Prince Phillip asked Princess Aurora one morning.

Aurora looked around the royal stable. There were so many horses! It was always hard to choose. But then she had an idea.

"From now on, I think I'd like to ride the same horse every day," Aurora said.

"What a wonderful idea," Phillip agreed. "You can have a horse of your own—just as I have Samson."

Aurora smiled. "And I've already decided which one," she said.

A fine palomino warhorse had caught Aurora's eye. He was the most beautiful creature she had ever seen!

A groom brought the horse out of his stall and put him through his paces. The horse was bold and proud and brave. He marched around the palace courtyard as confidently as if he were the king himself. He was amazing!

Aurora liked the horse even more when she rode him. "What's his name?" she asked the groom.

"We call him Brutus, Your Highness," the groom replied.

"Oh, no!" Aurora exclaimed. "That won't do at all. I think I'll call him . . . Buttercup."

Phillip and the groom looked surprised. "Er—are you sure?" Phillip asked.

Aurora smiled. "Do *you* like your new name, Buttercup?"

The horse snorted happily. He loved his new name!

46

Aurora rode Buttercup all around the castle grounds. When the pages blew their trumpets as they rode by, he didn't flinch. When a carriage rumbled past, he stood at attention. When Aurora asked him to jump over a stone wall, he cleared it effortlessly.

Aurora was thrilled. Buttercup was perfect!

The next day, Aurora decided to ride Buttercup out to the fairies' cottage so they could meet him.

"Why don't you let me saddle up Samson and come with you?" Phillip suggested, looking worried. "You shouldn't ride off through the woods all alone."

"Don't be silly," Aurora said with a laugh. "I grew up in those woods, remember? Besides, I won't be alone. I'll be with Buttercup. He'll take care of me!"

Aurora and Buttercup pranced off across the grounds. But the moment they entered the woods, Buttercup became a different horse. His steps slowed to a crawl. His eyes bulged nervously. And when some of Aurora's little woodland friends appeared, Buttercup tried to spin around and run away!

"What's the matter, Buttercup?" Aurora exclaimed in surprise. "Why, there's nothing to be frightened of!"

She could hardly believe the change in her horse. He was even afraid to step over a branch on the trail.

And when she asked him to walk through
a forest stream, he nearly fainted!

By the time she reached the cottage, Aurora was feeling a bit frustrated. How could a horse who was so brave at the palace be so timid in the woods?

Flora, Fauna, and Merryweather hurried out of their cottage. "Oh, what a lovely pony!" Merryweather exclaimed.

"Yes, he's beautiful, dear," Fauna added.

54

Aurora sighed. "He *is* beautiful," she said. "But he seems to be
afraid of everything in the woods!"

"There, there." Flora smiled. "I'm sure it will be all right.
You'll just need to be patient with him, that's all."

"Yes, dear, be patient," Merryweather agreed. But she sounded distracted. She moved closer to get a better look at Buttercup. "What a nice coat he has!"

"And such shiny hooves," Fauna added.

"Though he might look even nicer if his hooves were blue," Merryweather mused.

Zap! She aimed her wand. Just like that, Buttercup's hooves turned blue!

"Oh, don't be silly!" Flora exclaimed. "A horse shouldn't have blue hooves. On the other hand, his coat might look prettier in pink. . . ."

Zap! Buttercup's hooves returned to their normal color. But the rest of him turned pink.

"Quit that!" Merryweather cried. "Blue!"

"Pink!" Flora argued back.

Zap! Zap!

As the two fairies argued, the horse changed from one color to the next. Buttercup looked confused.

Aurora just sighed as she watched her new horse change colors. *That* didn't seem to bother him at all. But when a stray leaf fluttered down, he jumped and snorted as if it were a horse-eating dragon.

What was she going to do? She didn't want to give up on him. Buttercup was so perfect in every other way. Why did he have to be so skittish in the forest?

Soon it was time to say good-bye to the fairies. Aurora did her best to ignore the way Buttercup jumped and cringed at every shadow and leaf along the way. She had been certain that Buttercup was the perfect horse for her. But now she wasn't as sure.

Aurora was so deep in thought that she wasn't paying attention to anything else. But she looked up when Buttercup suddenly stopped dead in his tracks.

"What is it *this* time?" she asked with a sigh.

Then Aurora looked at the trail ahead . . . and gasped in horror. An enormous mountain lion was blocking their path!

Oh, no! Aurora's heart raced with fright as she watched the creature creep closer. If Buttercup could be scared of a bunny rabbit, he was certain to go crazy over a mountain lion. They were in trouble!

But this time, to Aurora's surprise, Buttercup didn't panic or try to run. Instead, he stood proudly and puffed himself up to look even bigger than he was. He planted his hooves and snorted angrily at the mountain lion.

Then he marched forward and struck out at the lion
with his front hooves! Aurora hung on. She was still scared.
But it seemed that Buttercup wasn't!

Buttercup's lack of fear made Aurora feel braver. She reached out and grabbed a sturdy tree branch.

"Leave us alone!" she yelled at the mountain lion, waving the branch. "Or else!"

Buttercup pawed at the ground and added a fierce snort to back up Aurora's words.

When the mountain lion didn't budge, Buttercup leaped forward
and pinned its tail to the ground with one hoof. Then Aurora reached
out and gave the lion a smart rap on the nose with her branch.

The lion didn't like that at all. It let out an embarrassed yowl.
Then it yanked its tail free and raced away into the woods.

Aurora was pleased with herself—and with her horse. Buttercup had been brave when it really counted.

"Come on, Buttercup," she said, giving him a pat. "Let's go home."

Buttercup snorted again, proudly, and pranced off.

As Aurora and Buttercup neared the castle, a butterfly fluttered past. Buttercup's eyes went wide, and he jumped in terror.

But this time, Aurora just smiled. "You helped me feel brave when it was most important, Buttercup," she told him. "Now maybe I can help you get past your fears, too."

Aurora stroked Buttercup's neck and talked to him in a soft voice, reminding him to stay calm. The butterfly fluttered closer and closer . . . and finally landed right on his nose (which was only shaking a *little*).

"Good boy!" she praised him. "You know, Buttercup, I think we make a perfect team!"

DISNEY's Aladdin

The Desert Race

Princess Jasmine and Aladdin were strolling across the palace grounds one fine evening when the Sultan came running out onto a balcony.

"Drat!" the Sultan cried. "Oh, drat, drat, drat that dratted Desert Race!"

Jasmine was surprised. Usually her father loved the Desert Race! Every year, the best riders from Agrabah competed against those of the neighboring kingdom of Zagrabah. The fastest horse and rider were awarded the prized Golden Palm trophy.

"What's the matter, Father?" Jasmine asked.

The Sultan shook his head sadly. "I just heard that Prince Fayiz will be riding for Zagrabah again. Drat! His horse is so fast that he's won the last three years in a row!"

"I have an idea, Father!" Jasmine said eagerly. "I could ride my horse Midnight in the Desert Race this year. He's the fastest horse in Agrabah!"

"Oh, dear me, no!" The Sultan looked shocked at the very suggestion. "The Desert Race can be dangerous. I won't have my daughter risking her neck like that!"

"How about if *I* ride Midnight in the race?" Aladdin spoke up.

The Sultan's face brightened immediately. "What a splendid idea!" he cried. "You'll have such fun, my boy!"

Aladdin had never ridden Midnight before. In fact, nobody but Jasmine had ever ridden him. So the next day they went to the stables to give Aladdin and Midnight a chance to get to know each other. However, Midnight wouldn't even let Aladdin groom him!

When Aladdin came toward him with the saddle, Midnight jumped out of reach.

"Let me help," Jasmine said. Midnight gave her no trouble at all—as usual. Soon the horse was ready to go.

"No big deal," Aladdin muttered. "The Desert Race is about riding, not grooming and saddling." He swung onto Midnight's back.

But Midnight still wasn't ready to cooperate. He kicked up his heels and sent Aladdin flying!

Aladdin brushed himself off. "Okay, let's try this again. . . ." he said. But it was no use. Midnight just wouldn't let Aladdin ride him!

Jasmine was getting worried. Was there something wrong with her horse?

"Maybe he's not feeling well," she said. "Here, let me try."
Midnight stood like a rock while Jasmine climbed into the saddle. Then he happily carried her all around the stable yard, doing everything she asked.

Jasmine shrugged and smiled. "Sorry," she told Aladdin. "I guess Midnight is a one-person horse."

"*Now* how are we supposed to win that trophy back?" the Sultan asked.

"Let me ride in the race, Father," Jasmine urged. "I can do it!"

The Sultan didn't seem to hear her. "Well, perhaps one of the other Agrabah riders will surprise everyone this year," he said. "Or perhaps we can find Aladdin another fast horse." He didn't look very hopeful, though.

"Don't worry," Aladdin said. "I'll think of something. . . ."

The day of the race arrived. Riders from Zagrabah paraded into Agrabah with a servant carrying the Golden Palm leading the way. Behind him rode Fayiz on his impressive gray stallion, Desert Warrior.

"I don't know why we bothered to bring it with us," Fayiz said haughtily, gesturing at the trophy. "We'll only have to carry it all the way back to Zagrabah again after the race."

When it was time for the race, fans from Agrabah jostled with visitors from Zagrabah for the best views. Fayiz and his horse looked confident as they took their spot at the starting line.

The Sultan watched as Aladdin joined the line. "What an odd-looking horse that boy is riding," he remarked. "I wonder why I've never seen it before." But he didn't have time to worry about that. "Now, where is Jasmine?" he wondered aloud. "It's time to start the race!"

But Jasmine was nowhere to be found.

"Oh, well." The Sultan raised the starting flag, which was almost too heavy for him. "Can't wait any longer, I suppose. One, two, three—they're off!"

The riders galloped into the desert, heading for the oasis, which was the first landmark of the race.

A black horse with a mysterious veiled rider took the lead right away. As soon as they were out of view of the palace, the rider threw off the veil. It was Jasmine!

"I do hate going against Father's wishes," she whispered to Midnight. "But I just had to prove that you were the fastest."

Aladdin was riding right behind the black horse as the racers neared the oasis. He was curious about the rider. Who could it be? He urged his horse forward and finally got a look.

"Jasmine!" he gasped, though nobody could hear him over the pounding hooves.

Aha! He'd thought that black horse looked familiar. . . .

Aladdin opened his mouth to call out to Jasmine. But just then, his horse spotted the cool, inviting water of the oasis.

"Now *that's* more like it!" the horse exclaimed. Only it wasn't really a horse—it was the Genie!

"Hey! This wasn't part of the plan!" Aladdin cried as the Genie transformed from a horse into a sea horse and dove right into the water.

"Don't worry, Al," the Genie said happily. "We'll catch up. Gotta stay hydrated, you know!"

Aladdin watched helplessly as Jasmine and Midnight galloped off without a backward glance.

Jasmine and Midnight had been in the lead since the race began. Most of the other horses were falling farther behind. But Fayiz and Desert Warrior were starting to catch up. Jasmine urged her horse on, but Midnight couldn't seem to pull away. Warrior was big, strong, and very fast. Finally, he edged ahead of Midnight.

"Give up now!" Fayiz shouted. "That trophy will always belong to Zagrabah!"

But Midnight wasn't finished yet. He surged forward again . . . and passed Warrior!

"Not so fast!" Jasmine called to Fayiz with a laugh. "That trophy is in Agrabah today. And that's where it's going to stay!"

Fayiz gritted his teeth. He looked determined, and Warrior wasn't giving up, either. They stayed right at Midnight's heels . . . until the horses had to jump a ditch that crossed the path.

Midnight sailed over easily, but Warrior skidded to a stop!

With Fayiz and Warrior out of the running, it seemed there was nothing to keep Jasmine and Midnight from winning. But then Jasmine heard the sound of hoofbeats close behind her!

"What?" she cried, looking back.

It was Aladdin! Jasmine was amazed. She didn't even know he was in the race! And where did he get that fast—but very strange looking—horse?

Soon Aladdin and his mystery horse had caught up, and he and Jasmine were fighting for the lead. Jasmine was glad that the trophy would stay in Agrabah no matter which one of them won. But she *really* wanted to prove that Midnight was the fastest horse in the two kingdoms. She urged him on.

The two horses were neck and neck as they neared the finish line. First Midnight pulled ahead a tiny bit, then it was Aladdin's horse. But neither could keep the lead . . .

. . . And so, the two horses crossed the finish line in a dead heat!

As soon as Midnight slowed to a stop, Jasmine jumped off, gave her tired horse a hug, and led him to the water trough for a drink.

"Excellent work, you two!" the Sultan cried. He was beaming as he ran over and hugged both Jasmine and Midnight. Then he frowned. "Er, wait," he said. "Didn't I forbid you to ride?"

"I'm sorry, Father," Jasmine began. "It's just that—"

"Oh, never mind," the Sultan interrupted with a grin. "Agrabah is victorious at last! Twice over, in fact!"

Jasmine walked over to Aladdin.

"Congratulations!" Aladdin said when he saw her coming.

"Same to you," Jasmine replied. "But where in the world did you find yourself such a fast horse?

"Er . . ." Aladdin said, looking at his horse. Then he looked at his feet. "Um, that is . . ." He didn't seem to know what to say.

"Surprise!" the Genie cried, transforming back into his usual form.

Jasmine gasped. "Genie? That was *you*?"

"Sorry, Princess," the Genie said, winking. "We were just *horsing* around."

Aladdin grinned sheepishly. "It was my idea. I couldn't bear the thought of Zagrabah winning again this year."

The Sultan had overheard the whole thing. "Oh, dear," he said with a frown. "The rules state that it must be a horse-and-rider team—not a *genie*-and-rider team! I'm afraid this disqualifies you two from the race." Then he smiled. "And that means Jasmine and Midnight are the winners!"

Jasmine patted Midnight proudly as she rode him in the victory parade. She had always known he was fast. But she'd never imagined he was so fast that he could match a genie for speed!